MIRRORED

THE NIGHTMARE CLUB

MIRRORED

ANNIE GRAVES

ILLUSTRATED BY
GLENN MCELHINNEY

MINNEAPOLIS

First published in Dublin, Ireland by Little Island
Original edition © Little Island 2011

American edition © 2015 Darby Creek,
a division of Lerner Publishing Group, Inc.

Darby Creek
A division of Lerner Publishing Group, Inc.
241 First Avenue North
Minneapolis, MN 55401 USA

For reading levels and more information, look up this title
at www.lernerbooks.com.

Main body text set in ITC Stone Serif Std. 11.5/15.
Typeface provided by Adobe Systems.

Library of Congress Cataloging-in-Publication Data

Graves, Annie.
    Mirrored / by Annie Graves ; illustrated by Glenn
McElhinney.
        pages   cm. — (The Nightmare Club)
    Originally published: Dublin, Ireland : Little Island,
2011.
    ISBN: 978–1–4677–4349–5 (lib. bdg : alk. paper)
    ISBN: 978–1–4677–7636–3 (eBook)
    [1. Mirrors—Fiction. 2. Horror stories.] I.
McElhinney, Glenn, illustrator. II. Title.
PZ7.G77512Mi 2015
[Fic]—dc23   2014015438

Manufactured in the United States of America
1 – SB – 12/31/14

For Mum and Dad ... wherever you are!

Annie Graves is twelve years old, and she has no intention of ever growing up. She is, conveniently, an orphan, and lives at an undisclosed address in the Glasnevin area of Dublin, Ireland, with her pet toad, Much Misunderstood, and a small black kitten, Hugh Shalby Nameless. You needn't think she goes to school—pah!—or has anything as dull as brothers and sisters or hobbies, but let's just say she keeps a large cauldron on the stove.

This is not her first book. She has written eight so far, none of which is her first.

Publisher's note: We did try to take a picture of Annie, but her face just kept fading away. We have sent our camera for investigation but suspect the worst.

THANK You!

Let's face it, this is *my* book and *I* wrote it and I couldn't have done it without myself. But I suppose I'd better thank Alice Stevens, who helped a teeny bit and seems to frighten people without trying that hard.

Thanks to Kevin Stevens, too, for dropping Alice off at the Nightmare Club. Who said parents are good for nothing? (Oh, yeah, that was me—hah!)

I t's me, Annie. Hey!

I'm the nice one. The rest of them are all right, I suppose, but I'm the one people *really* like.

Some say it's my great big witchy house they like. Some say it's my deep, dark, spidery basement with the window that keeps opening and closing no matter how tightly I latch it.

Others say it's really Hugh Shalby Nameless, my very own black kitten, that people like.

I know it can't be Much Misunderstood, my pet toad, because everyone hates him, except me.

Anyway, whatever the reason, they all come here every year, every Halloween, for a sleepover, and we have the Nightmare Club.

We all huddle in our sleeping bags (some of them bring their *teddies,* but I pretend not to notice), and we tell each other ghosty stories deep into the night and we scare each other half to DEATH!

The Nightmare Club is all about having nightmares and telling about your nightmares and giving everyone else nightmares.

I maybe forgot to mention the "true rule." The stories are supposed to be true. Because that's much scarier than fake stuff. That's why stories about witches and ghosts aren't really allowed.

I made a new rule this year. We all have to whisper. I tell them it's so my mum and dad can't hear us. But you know that's not true because I ... sort of ... *mislaid* my mum and dad ...

But, the thing is, stories are scarier when they are told in whispers, aren't they? I don't know why that is...

So you have to imagine this story being told in a whisper.

And Karen's got *such* a creepy whisper.

There was this girl in my class called Abbey. We used to be friends.

I liked her 'cause she invented the best games. My favorite was when we made potions and cast spells on the boys in our class. I was just pretending, but Abbey would get really into it, like it was real.

The other kids in our class thought she was weird and didn't really talk to her. But I thought she was more fun than anyone else in school.

But after last summer, Abbey was different. She never played games anymore. When I asked her if she wanted to play virtual rollercoaster, she looked at me like she had a bad taste in her mouth.

Suddenly, Abbey was popular. All the kids wanted to be her friend. But I didn't. I thought she was boring now. And she was kind of mean. She was the one who made fun of the "weird" kids now.

Then a rumor started going around school about why Abbey changed. I don't know if it's true, but I have to tell somebody...

Even at home, Abbey didn't really have anyone to talk to.

Her parents acted like she wasn't there.

Her older brother, Pearse, treated her like a little kid because he was in high school and knew how to do algebra and speak Spanish.

So Abbey read lots of stories. Stories about princesses and acrobats and pirates and explorers.

And she was a really great painter. Big, colorful pictures of jungles and oceans and castles.

But mostly, she liked to play make-believe. She was a sorceress or a liontamer or the queen of a country where all the boys were slaves.

One time she invented special night goggles and made wings out of ostrich feathers, and she flew all over the world, looking into the houses of rich people and film stars.

But Abbey had no one to play with. I was her only friend in school, and at home she had no sisters or friends in the neighborhood.

So, when summer came, she was by herself.

One day Abbey was playing in her bedroom. She was an astronaut, Abbey Armstrong, on the surface of Zortek, a strange and dangerous planet.

Suddenly she thought she saw something move out of the corner of her eye. She spun around. It was only her reflection in the mirror.

Oh, this make-believe. Now her own
reflection was giving her the spooks.

But then something *really* weird
happened. Her reflection smiled at her.

Abbey wasn't smiling.

And her reflection
began to talk!

"Hello, Abbey."

Abbey couldn't
believe it! She opened
her eyes wide.

"Abbey, don't be scared. My name is Bee.
I'm just like you."

Abbey finally stuttered, "No—you *are* me."

Bee grinned. "That's what you're *supposed* to think. I follow your every move so quickly, you think it's your own. I look like you, I change when you change, I blink when you blink, I speak when you speak. But I'm not you."

Bee was whispering, and *her* eyes were wide open.

"I live in an *entirely* different world—the world of mirrors. We copy people so they never know we're here."

Abbey's heart was beating really quickly.
She was curious. Another world!

This was like a fantasy come true!

"What's your world like?" she asked.

Bee sat cross-legged on the floor. She told Abbey to sit down, too.

"You see, you think I'm a reflection. But it's just a trick to hide *our* world. I'm real, like you."

"Outside *my* bedroom is a world made of glass. Glass that never breaks. Even the *people* are glass. It's really beautiful."

Abbey was amazed. A glass world!

"Now, we're *supposed* to copy everything people do when they look in a mirror," Bee said. "But I'm so *bored* with that. I'm sick of pretending I don't exist. I wanted to meet you, Abbey, and learn about your world."

Abbey and Bee became great friends.
Abbey told Bee about her boring school
and her parents and Pearse and the kids
who didn't get her.

Bee told Abbey about the times when
Pearse came into her room when she
wasn't there and tried to find her diary
so he could read it.

She also told her about the world of glass,
entire glass cities stretching for miles.
About the sparkling buildings. People who
looked like ice sculptures. Orange skies
above a lemon street.

Abbey loved Bee. She was just like her. She understood Abbey in a way that no one else could.

She could tell Bee her secrets. She knew Bee would never betray her.

And Bee could watch her room for her.

You never knew what Pearse would do.
He was such a sneak.

Abbey told Bee about how Pearse never
had time for her. He treated her like a
child and teased her whenever she said
anything.

Abbey had found a best friend, a twin.
At her house. In her room!

Then, one Saturday afternoon, Abbey ran into her room sobbing. Pearse had made fun of one of her best drawings. Things like this were always happening in the Street family. When she got upset, her parents told her to stop being silly.

She was so angry!

She ran to Bee and told her all about it.
"I wish I could get out of here. Sometimes
I *hate* them. I wish I could be someplace
different," she sniffed. "Somewhere away
from *them.*"

Bee looked at Abbey and said softly, "You know, Abs, there is *something* you could do."

Abbey stopped sniffing. "What?"

"You could come in here."

"Oh," Abbey cried, *"could* I?"

"Of course."

"Really, Bee?! I could?"

"Of course, Abs. You're my best friend." They grinned at each other and burst out laughing.

"But one thing," Bee said. "I'd have to come out there. That's the only way it would work."

Abbey made a face. "Pearse would think you were me. He would be so mean to you."

"Don't you worry about that." Bee smiled. "I can handle Pearse."

Abbey and Bee agreed to swap the next afternoon. Just for a couple of hours.

Abbey could hardly sleep that night.
What an adventure. Like flying around
the world in night goggles. But this
was *real*.

After lunch Bee and Abbey faced each other in the mirror. Both of them were serious and nervous.

"OK, Bee, here we go." Abbey stepped forward and reached to touch Bee's hands through the mirror. She took a deep breath.

Abbey felt a strange, cold sensation like she was passing through icy water. She came out on the other side of the mirror.

It was very weird. Everything was opposite. The letters of her name above her bed were backward. Abbey turned back to the mirror.

Bee had opened the window and stuck
her head out. She looked almost crazy.
She turned to Abbey and grinned. "This is
brilliant. See you later, Abs—good luck."

She closed the window, ran out the door,
and slammed it behind her.

Abbey waited for her heart to stop
pounding. She went to the window,
but she couldn't open it. It was
stuck fast.

And a funny thing—all she could see outside was her own back garden, only in reverse. No glass buildings. No people like ice sculptures. No orange skies.

She would have to go out into the street
and have a look. Everything was only a
reflection in here. Out there, beyond that
bedroom door with the handle on the
wrong side, was a new world.

She checked her clock. It was backwards,
but she figured out that it was two
o'clock. They were supposed to meet
back here at teatime.

Abbey walked over to her bedroom door and grabbed the handle.

It was stuck. She twisted it again, but it wouldn't move—not even a little bit. She jerked it harder and harder, pushed at the door, banged it in frustration. Finally she gave up.

She tried the window again but couldn't budge it. This was really annoying. She'd have to wait for Bee to come back and explain how to work the door. How could she not have mentioned this?

Abbey sat down in a huff and waited for Bee. Hours passed. Teatime came and went, but she didn't return. Abbey was hungry. And cold.

She tried to read, but the writing in her books was backwards.

Finally, the door opened. Bee must be coming back!

But it wasn't Bee. It was Pearse. If he saw her, everything would be ruined!

She tried to hide, but it was too late!
Pearse walked up to the mirror and looked
right at her. She froze.

But he did what he always did when
he looked in any mirror. He raised his
arms and started flexing his muscles. He
couldn't see her! He was looking at his
own reflection!

Abbey giggled and stuck her tongue out at him from behind the glass.

Abbey's mother called Pearse. He jumped and ran out the door, shutting it behind him.

How strange—no one could see her in the mirror. It was like she was invisible. Abbey thought it was kind of cool, but it also worried her.

No one knew she was here.

And where on earth was Bee?

But Bee still didn't come, and it was way past teatime. Abbey tried the door a few more times. Nothing. And she was cold. So she climbed into bed and waited.

Eventually she dozed off.

She woke to a bang. It was dark outside and dark in the room. She tried the lamp, but it wouldn't turn on.

She peered through the mirror in the dark and made out the shape of someone at the door. "Bee," she whispered. Abbey was really frightened.

But Bee didn't answer her.

Bee ignored her. Then she put on a nightdress—Abbey's favorite blue nightdress—and got into bed.

"Bee!" Abbey was screaming now. "Look at me! *Look at me!"*

But Bee was asleep—or maybe she was pretending to be asleep.

Abbey shouted and screamed. In the dark. In the cold.

She slumped to the floor, exhausted.

Suddenly the lights were blazing. And there was Bee, staring through the mirror.

Abbey leaped to her feet.

"Oh, Bee, I was so frightened."

"Why, Abbey? What's wrong?"

"It's cold in here and everything's backwards," she said in a rush, "and you told me about glass buildings and glass people and everything, but outside it looks the same, and I can't even open the door to go outside."

"Of course you can't open the door. The mirror world can *only* reflect your world. My world is only a reflection. There's nothing else."

Abbey looked at Bee in horror. "But what about the houses and cities and parks made of glass?"

"Don't be stupid, Abs, that's not real. It's make-believe. And you love make-believe, don't you?"

Abbey felt suddenly cold, even colder than she had felt lying on the floor.

"So let me out," she said. "Let's swap back."

Bee laughed at her. "I don't think so, Abs."

"Why?"

She smiled the most evil smile you could imagine. "It's my turn to be Abbey now."

With that, she walked back to bed and climbed in.

When she leaned over to switch off the light, she was still smiling.

Then all was black.

Now, it's probably just a story. At least I hope it is.

The older kids probably made it up to scare us.

The only thing is . . . I saw Abbey in the bathroom one day. And I'm sure that when she passed the mirrors, I couldn't see her reflection.

THE END

EEEEEEEK!
I really want to
scream after that.

I want to scream
and scream and scream
to drown out the sounds of
Abbey screaming, but I know she will just
go on screaming in my head and I will
never, ever, EVER sleep again.

EVER.

Unless someone else tells me another
story to take my mind off it . . .

Check out
all the titles in

THE
NIGHTMARE
CLUB

MIRRORED

ANNIE GRAVES

THE NIGHTMARE CLUB

GUINEA PIG KILLER

ANNIE GRAVES

THE NIGHTMARE CLUB

FRANKENKIDS

ANNIE GRAVES

THE NIGHTMARE CLUB

THE WOLFLING'S BITE

ANNIE GRAVES

THE NIGHTMARE CLUB

THE DEMON BABYSITTER

ANNIE GRAVES

THE NIGHTMARE CLUB

THE HATCHING

ANNIE GRAVES

THE NIGHTMARE CLUB